AN

ANNA
THE WITCH

BOOK!

A BOOK OF MISCHIEF AND MAGIC ...

MARIAN BRODERICK was born in north London to Irish parents, and still lives in the same street where she grew up. She couldn't read until she was eight years old but once she started, she couldn't stop. At nine, she wrote a series of detective stories, which luckily have been lost in the cellar of her house. As an adult, Marian became a book editor, working for publishing companies in Britain, Ireland, Australia, Hong Kong and Japan. She has written several books for children, including *The Lost Fairy* and the first two books in the 'Anna the Witch' series, *The Witch Apprentice* and *The Witch in the Woods*. Is she a witch? Well, she does have two cats …

'ANNA THE WITCH' BOOKS

THE WITCH APPRENTICE

THE WITCH IN THE WOODS

A WITCH IN A FIX

A WITCH IN A FIX

MARIAN BRODERICK

ILLUSTRATED BY FRANCESCA CARABELLI

THE O'BRIEN PRESS
DUBLIN

For my darling Conall, the most magical of all creatures.

First published 2009 by The O'Brien Press Ltd,
12 Terenure Road East, Rathgar, Dublin 6, Ireland.
Tel: +353 1 4923333; Fax: +353 1 4922777
Email: books@obrien.ie
Website: www.obrien.ie

ISBN: 978 1 04717 130 6

British Library Cataloguing-in-Publication Data
A catalogue record for this title is available from the British Library

1 2 3 4 5 6 7 8 9

09 10 11 12 13

The O'Brien Press
receives assistance from

Layout and design: The O'Brien Press
Printed and bound in the UK by CPI Group Ltd.

CONTENTS

I

MRS CUFFY

All the teachers at St Munchin's are really cool. I especially like Mrs Winkle, the head, but I've got a good reason for that, as you will see.

The only one who's a problem is Mrs Cuffy, my science teacher. Actually she's more than a problem. I think she hates me. And I'm not mad keen on her either.

I'm not the only one who feels this way. Mrs Cuffy is the nastiest teacher in the whole school and we're *all* scared of her!

She has long, stringy brown hair just like rats' tails, and a pointed twitchy nose. And, I swear, she has a straggly black moustache!

It's bad luck that we don't get on, because Mrs Winkle says I've got to get good at science. You see, Mrs Winkle knows something about me that very few people know.

She knows that I, Anna Kelly, am a witch! And the reason she knows this is simple. It's because Mrs Winkle, as well as being our head teacher, is also a witch!

Of course I'm only a junior witch – an apprentice. But Mrs Winkle is an expert witch and she is helping to train me.

She says that science *should* be one of my best subjects. In fact, she says I can't be a proper witch without natural science. I need to know all about plants and biology and why things in nature behave the way they do.

But there's a problem: it's boring! I don't like science experiments out of books. I hate testing whether plants sweat and whether a coin is heavier than a cork in water.

Instead, I like doing *magic* experiments that come out of my head! And what I'm *really* into is a type of magic I can do called 'shape-shifting'.

Shape-shifting is fantastic. No books, no test tubes. All you have to do is point at something, concentrate, and make up a magical rhyme.

Then the thing you're pointing at turns into whatever you want, like an animal or vegetable or anything!

* * *

So there I was last Monday afternoon, sitting beside my friend Mary in the science lab. I was gazing out of the window – and I was bored out of my tiny, weeny brain.

I was daydreaming about flying out of the window when suddenly a screech like a banshee shattered my thoughts *and* my eardrums.

'Anna Kelly!' shouted Mrs Cuffy. 'Come to the front this minute!'

I shot up straight in my seat and met Mrs Cuffy's beady little black eyes. Mary looked at me sideways.

'You're for it now,' she whispered.

'Thanks,' I said.

Mrs Cuffy stood at the front of the class with her thin lips curling in disgust. In her hand, she held one corner of a dirty piece of paper, waving it about as if it was an old snotrag. I took a deep

breath and dragged myself up to face her.

'And what,' she shouted, twitching her moustache, 'do you call this?'

'My homework?' I said.

'Cheek!' she snapped. 'Detention tonight for being cheeky!'

I gasped. I wasn't being cheeky! The snotraggy-looking scrap *was* my homework – it wasn't *my* fault it ended up looking like that. My cat Charlie had eaten his dinner off it when I wasn't looking.

'But Miss,' I said. 'It *is* my homework. Look!'

I pointed at the untidy squiggles that were meant to be yet another experiment about the effects of vinegar on eggshells. It wasn't very good, but I'd done my best.

'Anna Kelly,' said Mrs Cuffy. 'This is meant to

be a simple science experiment about weak acids, not an explosion in a catfood factory! You'll write it out again after school – twice! Sit down!'

I trailed back to my desk and sat down. It wasn't fair. Out of the whole class, she always picked on me – and I was sick of it! Mary squeezed my arm and smiled at me in sympathy. The bell rang for the end of class and everyone leapt out of their seats.

'Freeze!' shouted Mrs Cuffy, and everyone froze. 'Mary Maxwell, you will stay behind for smirking at Anna Kelly. The rest of you may all file out in an orderly fashion!'

Mary's mouth fell open in shock.

'But I … but I wasn't smirking!' she stammered.

'Double detention for cheek!' shouted Mrs Cuffy. 'Go and see Mrs Winkle right now, and tell her I sent you!'

Poor Mary went bright red and her eyes welled with tears as she walked slowly out of the classroom in front of the hushed boys and girls. She was supposed to be in a gym competition tonight, and now she would miss it – all because of rat-faced, whiskery Mrs Cuffy!

And that was what did it. That was what finally made my blood boil. I'm not proud of it, but there and then I decided to do something drastic. I was going to teach Mrs Cuffy a lesson!

2

ANNA TEACHES A LESSON

I waited until the last person had left the class-room. Mrs Cuffy and I were alone. She plonked herself into her chair and took out a magazine. I shot my hand into the air.

'Miss?' I said. 'Please can I come to the front and collect my homework?'

'Too dim to do it from memory, are we?' said Mrs Cuffy. 'Very well. But *don't* disturb me again – and *don't* speak to that little friend of yours when she comes back. I hope Mrs Winkle gives her what for!'

I pressed my lips together, slipped a pencil into my pocket and crept towards Mrs Cuffy's desk. I took my fishy-smelling homework from the pile – and dropped it on the floor on purpose.

'Clumsy clot!' said Mrs Cuffy. Her beady little

eyes stared at me for a second and then she went back to reading her magazine.

I dropped down onto my knees to make her think I was picking up my homework – but really I was quickly drawing a small five-

pointed magic star on the floor with my pencil!

When I'd finished, I stood up and stepped inside the star. I put my hands on my hips, took a deep breath and waited. Mrs Cuffy glanced up at me and glared. Her moustache twitched with irritation.

'Anna Kelly!' she shouted. 'What *do* you think you're doing, standing there like an idiot? Get back to your seat at once!'

'I *will* go back to my seat, Mrs Cuffy,' I said. 'But not until you promise to let Mary go to gym instead of detention, *and* say sorry for making her cry!'

'Say *sorry*!' spluttered Mrs Cuffy, dropping her magazine in shock. 'Apologise to a pupil? *Me*? Are you mad?'

I squared my shoulders.

'What you did wasn't fair, Mrs Cuffy,' I said. 'And I'm giving you one last chance to make amends!'

'*You* are giving *me* a chance?' said Mrs Cuffy slowly, as if she couldn't believe her ears. Then she leapt out of her chair.

'How dare you!' she shouted. 'I've never been spoken to like that in my life!' She picked up a ruler and advanced towards me.

I caught my breath. Surely she wasn't going to *clobber* me!

'It's about time you got what we used to call six of the best, my girl!' she said. 'Six of the best wallops I can give you!'

That was going too far. Detention is one thing but even *I* know that hitting is wrong. It was time for Plan B.

I planted my two feet firmly in the magic star, pointed my finger at Mrs Cuffy and said the first rhyme that came into my head.

'Unkind Cuffy, cruel to kids,
Watch me put your life on skids!
Grow a rodent's tail and paws
And slink around upon all fours!'

Straight away I felt the power of magic surging from the floor beneath me. It shot through my legs, into my whole body, and out through the finger that pointed at Mrs Cuffy. A blue flash of light blinded me.

When the smoke cleared, sitting on the chair where Mrs Cuffy had been, was a large, greasy brown RAT!

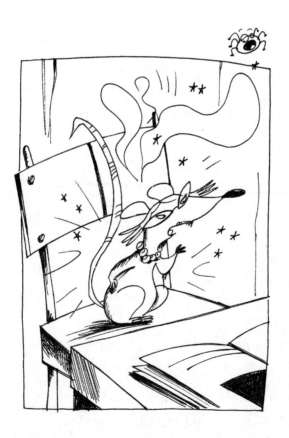

3

RAT IN THE CLASSROOM!

The rat – Mrs Cuffy – skittered about on the chair, and I jumped up and down on the spot laughing my head off. *This* was more like it! Who needed science out of books – or science teachers!

But about three seconds later, I heard footsteps coming up the hall. Then it hit me. What on earth had I done? And, more importantly, what was I going to do *now*?

The footsteps were coming closer. It had to be Mary, already on her way back from Mrs Winkle's office.

Now, even though she was my best friend, Mary didn't know I was a witch. I always kept school and witchcraft separate and never told anyone in case they all treated me like a total weirdo.

If I let her in, she was bound to ask where Mrs Cuffy was – and then she would see the rat and faint or something …

'Rats! – I mean, blast!' I whispered, gazing at Mrs Cuffy. She made a furious chattering sound, crossed her little ratty arms, and tapped one foot. Her black eyes glittered at me.

Quick as I could, I jumped back inside my magic star, pointed at her again and chanted:

'Lose your snout, your tail, your fur,
And change back into what you were!'

Nothing happened – except Mrs Cuffy squeaked and chattered even louder. I'd have to think of something else. I rushed to the door and tried to block Mary.

'Mary!' I said, draping my arm across the doorway. '*So* nice to see you again!'

'Mrs Winkle said I had to do as I was told,' she said glumly. She looked at me with red-rimmed eyes. 'I suppose we'd better get on with it, or we'll be in even more trouble.'

'Good news!' I said. 'Mrs Cuffy changed her mind – we're off the hook!'

'What?' she said. 'What do you mean, *off the hook*?'

'No detention,' I said. 'Mrs Cuffy's busy.'

'Are you *sure*?' said Mary, looking confused. 'It's not like her to miss a chance to inflict a punishment.'

'Yep,' I said. 'After you left, she droned on at me for a while – but then she said we had to go home! Straight away. Right now. Without delay.'

I could hardly believe how many lies were tripping so easily out of my mouth. Mary tried to peep over my shoulder.

caretaker?'

'No need for that,' I said. I picked up her bag and dragged her down the corridor. 'Do you want to be here all night and miss gym?'

That did the trick. Mary Maxwell loved her gym.

'I suppose you're right,' she said. 'Ugh! Rats live in drains and rubbish tips, you know! I saw a programme about it on TV ...'

All the way out of school Mary yakked about rats and mice and cockroaches, but I was only half-listening.

I was in trouble. If Mrs Winkle found out I was turning her staff into animals, she would probably expel me – she might even strip me of all my witchy powers! My life would be ruined.

I needed to find a way of turning Cuffy-the-rat back into Cuffy-the-grouchy-science-teacher *without* Mrs Winkle knowing. And I needed to do it fast!

4

AT HOME AT CRAG ROAD

That evening at home at number 13 Crag
Road was very uncomfortable for me. I live
with my two aunts, who aren't witches themselves, but know a lot about witchcraft. They
encourage me in my magic studies.

So as soon as I stepped through the kitchen
door, I confessed what I'd done. I was *hoping*
they'd help me.

Fat chance! Instead of sympathising they
scolded me for *hours*. They were so busy lectur-
ing me, I didn't even get any tea. The only
member of the family who was nice to me was
my cat, Charlie!

'But WHY?' shouted Aunty Grizz for the tenth
time. 'What on earth made you do such a foolish,
wicked thing?!'

'Because Mrs Cuffy *always* picks on me!' I said. 'And today she even made Mary cry!'

'Anna, dear, *really*,' said Aunty Wormella. 'It's still going a little far, don't you think?'

'She deserved it,' I mumbled stubbornly. Charlie jumped onto my lap and snuggled down. At least *he* understood me.

'No one deserves to live life as a rodent!' shouted Aunty Grizz, thumping the kitchen table. She cast a pained look at an empty cage in a dusty corner of the kitchen. 'And *I* should know!'

It was true, she *did* know. Once a long time ago, in the days when I didn't like Aunty Grizz, I turned her into a mouse. I was just beginning to learn I had magic powers – and it was *thrilling*! But, of course, Aunty Grizz didn't see it quite like that.

'Do you have *any* idea what it's like to look at yourself in the mirror and realise you have big ears, four legs and a tail!' she shouted. 'And not in a good way!'

No, I had to admit, I had no idea how that might feel.

'And for all your talent, you couldn't change Grizz back, could you, dear,' said Aunty Wormella, shaking her head. 'She lived in that cage for weeks, eating nothing but toast crumbs. In the end, we had to call in Mrs Winkle to make her human again.'

My stomach did a back flip.

'But we can't call in Mrs Winkle this time!' I said, panicking. 'She'll skin me alive! She'll expel me! She'll turn *me* into something horrible …'

'You're already something horrible,' muttered Aunty Grizz, crossing her arms.

'Calm down, you two, calm down,' said Aunty Wormella. 'We'll never solve anything by losing our heads.'

'Hmph!' said Aunty Grizz. 'Sounds to me like she lost her head a long time ago. I blame you, Wormella, you've always spoiled the child …'

And off they went into an argument. They always did this. They could never agree on the best way to bring up an orphan witch, and whose fault it was that I was turning out so way-ward.

After about five minutes, I lost patience with the two of them. I took off my shoe and banged the table with it. Charlie jumped off my lap in fright and ran into his basket.

'*When* you've quite finished!' I said. 'We still have the small problem of my science teacher skulking around St Munchin's as a rat! *What* am I going to do?'

There was silence in the kitchen. The aunts looked at me and at each other. Aunty Grizz drummed the table with her fingers, while Aunty Wormella hummed a little tune under her breath. Finally Aunty Grizz sat up straight.

'Where is she now?' she asked.

'Don't know,' I said. Then I had an idea.

'*That's* what I have to do,' I said. 'Find her, coax her out of her hiding place, and turn her back into a human. Mrs Cuffy hasn't been a rat for very long. With a bit of luck, she won't remember anything about it.'

'But, Anna, dear,' Aunty Wormella said. 'You said you tried to change her back into a human when you were in class, but it didn't work.'

I waved my hands about airily.

'The heat of the moment,' I said. 'This time I'll find a really good spell. It'll be different when I get a chance to work on her properly.'

'And how are you supposed to find her, clever clogs?' asked Aunty Grizz.

We all sat scratching our heads and chins for a few silent minutes.

'I know!' said Aunty Wormella, clicking her fingers. 'The crystal ball! We haven't used it for ages! That'll tell you where she is!'

I'd forgotten we even had a crystal ball. At Crag Road, we still had a lot of equipment from the days when my aunts believed that *they* were the witches, and not me. We had cauldrons and broomsticks and pointy hats and jars of strange ingredients heaped in a jumble all over the house.

I don't use that sort of stuff – I don't even use a wand very often. I'm a modern witch – and all those old traditions and trappings are *soooo* last century! But, I must admit, they can come in handy sometimes – like now.

I scrambled onto the kitchen counter, reached to the top of a cupboard, and lifted down a dark red box with silver stars all over it. I hopped down and placed the box on the kitchen table. We all stood around and stared at it.

'Open it, then,' said Aunty Wormella, nudging me.

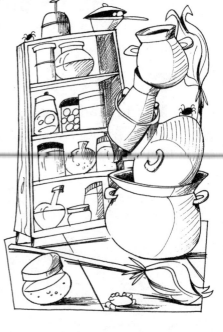

'OK, OK,' I said. I took the lid off the box and sifted through piles of scrunched-up newspaper. I felt something hard and cold, and lifted it out.

The crystal ball glittered as I placed it onto the kitchen table. I stared at it and shivered.

5

THE CRYSTAL BALL

The ball was about the size of a human head and made from pure sparkling crystal from Ancient Greece. It rested on a small circular stand made out of white sheep bones – at least, I *hoped* they were sheep bones. To one side there were several white knobs shaped like tiny human skulls.

'Get on with it, then!' said Aunty Grizz.

I closed my eyes and tried to remember what Mrs Winkle had taught me about operating a crystal ball. I spread my hands over it, took a deep breath and chanted:

'Crystal, crystal, please show me
Where the Cuffy-Rat could be!'

I opened my eyes. The crystal had clouded over. Inside the ball, all the colours of the rainbow swirled together, and tiny red sparks spat out from its middle. One of them hit Aunty Wormella on the hand.

'Ow!' she squeaked.

'Shhh!' said Aunty Grizz.

'Thanks for the sympathy,' replied Aunty Wormella.

As I gazed into

the ball, the colours cleared and a picture started to form. I could see a dark shape – a twitching shape with a long tail and whiskers …

'There she is!' I shouted. Charlie's ears pricked up. He trotted to the kitchen table and stood against it on his hind legs. When he saw the tasty big rat, he dribbled all over the floor.

'Go away, Charlie,' I said. 'She's not dinner, so you can forget about that!'

I peered into the ball. Mrs Cuffy was crouched in a small room. She was squeaking quietly to herself and ripping a pile of blue cloth to shreds with her sharp little teeth.

I twiddled the knobs. The picture zoomed out, and I saw that the room looked familiar. Very, VERY familiar …

I zoomed out a little more. No wonder! It was *my* room! At this very moment, Mrs Cuffy was in *my* bedroom in *our* house, vandalising my wardrobe!

'I don't believe it!' I said.

'Where is she? What's she doing?' said Aunty Wormella, peering over my shoulder.

'She's upstairs!' I said.

The two aunts leapt out of their seats and raced around the kitchen in a panic, bumping into each other and knocking things over.

'Go and catch her, Grizz!' shouted Aunty Wormella.

'*You* catch her, Wormella!' shouted Aunty Grizz.

'Where are the traps!' they both shouted at once, flinging open all the cupboard doors.

'Shh,' I said. 'Look at that! She's destroying my new jeans!'

'Dear me, Anna,' said Aunty Wormella, pausing. 'If Mrs Cuffy disliked you when she was human, she seems to dislike you even more now she's a rat!'

The aunts huddled behind me and we all stared at Mrs Cuffy's furtive movements. She suddenly looked up from her destructive work, stared straight at me, and hissed.

I drew back from the crystal ball. The image went wavy.

'You don't think she can see me, do you?' I whispered.

Aunty Grizz poked me sharply between the shoulder blades.

'Zoom in again,' she said. 'You're losing the picture.'

I sat forward and twiddled the knobs to zoom in. This time, behind Mrs Cuffy, I could see another dark shape moving slowly through the shadows of my room. What was *that*?

I twiddled the knobs again, but all I could see was a pair of golden eyes, unblinking, moving closer and closer to Mrs Cuffy …

Aunty Wormella glanced around the kitchen.

'Oh dear. I don't want to worry you, Anna,'

she said. 'But where's Charlie?'

I looked under the table. Charlie was nowhere to be seen. I swallowed hard and peered again at the dark shape with the golden eyes creeping through the darkness.

It was him, all right. He was upstairs trying to catch himself a late supper!

Mrs Cuffy suddenly stopped what she was doing. She twitched her ears and looked over her furry shoulder ...

At that moment, the crystal ball went cloudy and the pictures disappeared with a loud 'pop'.

6

MISSING TEACHER

The next morning, I sneaked into assembly late.

'Anna!' whispered Mary, beckoning me over. 'I've saved you a place.'

I slumped into the seat beside her.

There was a lot of activity in the school and there were police officers wandering about. But I was so exhausted I could hardly take it in.

I'd been running around the house and garden half the night, calling Charlie to come to me and trying to catch Mrs Cuffy before *he* caught her.

I failed at both. When Charlie finally appeared, it was after midnight, and he was waving his tail and licking his chops in a very suspicious way. Mrs Cuffy had disappeared again, leaving what had once been my new jeans as a pile of rags.

I hardly slept a wink after that, and by now I was panicking about whether Mrs Cuffy was alive or dead. This was all getting out of hand.

As usual on Tuesday mornings, it was assembly. Mrs Winkle's large, blue-suited figure stood on the stage at the front of the hall. All the staff sat in rows behind her. She raised her hands and looked very serious.

'Good morning, boys and girls,' she said. 'You may have noticed that the police are in school today.'

A buzz of chatter rippled around the hall.

'This is because our caretaker, Mr Cuffy, has reported that Mrs Cuffy did not return home last night!' said Mrs Winkle.

A gasp went around the school. Mary nudged me and I sank further into my chair.

'I expect you all to answer any questions the police may have, and give any help that you can,' said Mrs Winkle. 'Mr Cuffy, would you say a few words, please?'

Mr Cuffy got to his feet and came to the front.

He was a wiry little man with a flat nose and bright red cheeks. He looked like he was ready for a fight – but then he always looked like that.

'Mrs C was due home at 4.23pm,' he said. 'When she *still* hadn't appeared by 4.33pm and, I might add, there was no sign of my dinner, I took the obvious course of action. I rang the police.'

As he was speaking, I was distracted by a rustling sound at the side of the stage. My tired gaze wandered over to the red curtains. They seemed to be moving by themselves …

To my horror *and* relief, the next thing I saw was a whiskery, pointed nose poking out from underneath. It was Mrs Cuffy!

An excited ripple went around the whole school as, row by row, the children spotted her creeping out from under the curtain. It wasn't long before everyone erupted in screaming and pointing and laughter.

'Silence!' shouted Mrs Winkle, holding her arms aloft – but it was no good.

Mrs Cuffy shot right across the stage, and all the teachers hopped up on their chairs. Even

though she'd seen the rat before, Mary squealed louder than anyone.

But when Mrs Cuffy got to Mr Cuffy, she stopped and stared up at him. She stood on her hind legs, put her hands on her hips, and tapped her foot impatiently. Mr Cuffy, not knowing that the rat in front of him was, in fact, his wife, became extremely angry.

'What are you doing in my school, you dirty creature?' he shouted, purple with fury.

He whipped a scrubbing brush out of his overalls and hurled it at Mrs Cuffy. The scrubbing brush bopped her squarely on her head. She squealed in pain, and scampered down the stage steps towards the door.

As she passed where I was sitting, she paused. She lifted her ratty little paws to the side of her head, waggled them about – and blew a big, fat raspberry right at me!

Then she turned and raced out of the door into the playground. Mary grabbed my arm.

'That was the same rat *we* saw!' she said. 'You

don't see whiskers like that every day.' She looked at me out of the corner of her eye. 'What's it got against *you*?'

I didn't answer. This was embarrassing. It looked like Mrs Cuffy was deliberately trying to get me in trouble – and succeeding.

I caught Mrs Winkle's eye. She was staring straight down at me from the stage and frowning.

7

THE TRUTH SPELL

I was kicking a football against a fence in the playground when the dreaded message came.

'Anna!' said Mary, popping her head out of a nearby window. 'You're to go to Mrs Winkle's office immediately!'

'Thanks,' I said. 'Just what I needed.'

'What have you done?' said Mary. 'Is it something to do with that old rat?'

'Why would that have anything to do with me?' I said, quickly. 'It's probably because I was late today. Or something.'

'OK,' said Mary, drawing her head back in. 'Good luck.'

I booted the ball over the fence. I went inside and trailed down the hallway until I got to a closed door. On it was a sign in large, black letters:

Mrs Winkle
Head Teacher

I took a deep breath, knocked and entered.

'Well, well, well,' said Mrs Winkle, glancing up from her desk and fixing me to the spot with her blue-eyed gaze. 'If it isn't my special pupil, Anna Kelly.'

'Good morning, Mrs Winkle,' I said in a wobbly voice.

At school, no one but me knew that Mrs Winkle was not only a head teacher, but also a very senior witch. But even though no one knew that she had magic powers, everyone in school respected her. Her methods were what she called 'firm but fair', which basically meant you didn't mess her around.

But I was about to mess her around BIG-TIME. I was about to look her in the eye and tell lies – and that made me want to jump on the first plane to Australia.

I shifted from one foot to another and prayed I

wouldn't crack. She started off friendly enough.

'How are your magic studies going, Anna?' she said. 'Been to any interesting workshops lately?'

'No, Miss,' I said, trying to avoid her gaze. 'I've been studying at home mainly.'

'And what about your *practical* magic?' she said, peering over her glasses. 'Done any good experiments?'

My heart thumped loudly inside my chest.

'No, Miss,' I said, twisting the bottom of my jumper in my sweaty hands.

'Are you sure, Anna?' she said. 'No shape-shifting, for example? I know how fond you are of that particular trick.'

There was a pause.

'No, Miss,' I lied in a tiny voice.

Mrs Winkle rose out of her chair, and walked around to face me. She leant against a large silver box on her desk. I recognised that box because she used it sometimes when we were doing sorcery lessons together. It was her magic box – but what was it doing here? I gulped.

'It is very odd, don't you think?' she said. 'That you were the last person to see Mrs Cuffy last night?'

'That's not my fault!' I said.

'And then suddenly a very large rat shows up in school,' said Mrs Winkle, as if I hadn't spoken. 'Correct me if I'm wrong, but it seemed to take a dislike to you, Anna.'

'I don't know why that was, Miss,' I said. By now, my hands were dripping sweat onto the floor and I badly wanted to go to the loo.

Mrs Winkle watched me fidget and her eyes narrowed.

'You're hiding something from me, Anna,' she said. 'And that's very disappointing!'

I hung my head and felt my cheeks going red with shame. Upsetting Mrs Winkle was the last thing I wanted to do – but I couldn't tell her the truth, I just couldn't!

Mrs Winkle turned to the magic box and opened it.

'If you think, my dear young witch,' she said, 'that I'm not going to get to the bottom of this business, you can think again!'

She whipped around to face me – and I nearly jumped out of my skin. For in her hand she held a long silver wand – and she was pointing it right at *me*!

'Time for a little truth spell, I think,' she said.

My heart missed a beat.

'Mrs Winkle, *please*!' I whined. 'I *am* telling the truth!'

'No, Anna,' said Mrs Winkle. 'I'm afraid you're not!'

She raised her arms in the air and chanted:

'Meet my eyes and count to three
And in a heartbeat you will see
That, though you panic, prance or pout,
When I ask, the truth comes out!'

She fixed her blue eyes on me. I found I could *not* look away, try as I might! Immediately I felt my insides go swimmy, and my nose itch. Mrs Winkle's eyes bored into my brain, making it feel like jelly.

'One …' I said, dribbling slightly.

I didn't *want* to count to three – I just couldn't stop myself! This was strong magic from a true expert.

'Two…' I said.

I knew that after I said three, the next words out of me would be the whole story about Mrs Cuffy.

'Three!' I said. 'Last night, I—'

TAT-TAT-TAT-TAT!

The sound of loud knocking on the office door broke my trance. Mrs Winkle groaned. She took her eyes off mine and lowered her wand.

'Who is it?' she called.

'Police, madam,' a deep voice answered. 'Can we have a word?'

Mrs Winkle dropped her wand back into the magic box and bustled to the door. She opened it and I heard the sound of murmuring.

A truth spell needs eyeball-to-eyeball contact, so once Mrs Winkle wasn't staring at me, the magic started to drift off. I shook my head to clear my brain a little. That was close! But she'd be back in a minute …

I eyed the open magic box in front of me and the beautiful silver key on the table beside it. Mrs Winkle and the police officer were talking and no one was looking at me. I sneaked over to the box.

There just *had* to be something there that could help me – but *what*? I traced the pretty silver patterns with my fingers.

'Yes, officer, I'll come now,' said Mrs Winkle,

closing the door. 'Thank you.'

Rats! She was coming back. There was no time. I sprang away from the box.

'If you think you're off the hook, Anna, you can think again!' she said, frowning. 'But that's all for now.'

'Right, Miss,' I said, sighing with relief. 'Any time, Miss!'

She picked up the silver key and locked the magic box. She dropped the key in the top drawer of her desk.

'Out you go,' she said. 'I'm needed in the play-ground.'

'Yes, Miss,' I said. A new naughty plan started to form in my brain.

Mrs Winkle put on her raincoat, shooed me out of her office, and strode down the corridor without a backward glance.

I dawdled back to the playground thinking of the magic box – and about how I knew where the silver key was kept.

And, I'm ashamed to say, I smiled.

8

THE MAGIC BOX

*L*ater that night, I put on my trainers and stuffed an old witch's hat and a wand into a bag. My plan was to break into the school and find out if anything in Mrs Winkle's magic box could help me solve the problem of Mrs Cuffy.

There just *had* to be all sorts of cool stuff in that box! Maybe there was a potion to make you invisible! Or a spell to make you fly! Everyone said I was too young to do all that stuff yet – but no one could stop me if I was on my own, could they?

Of course, Charlie wanted to come too. He wound himself around my legs, pleading with his round golden eyes.

'No chance, Charlie,' I said, wagging my finger at him. 'This is not a job for a cat! You'd only try and gobble her up, you *know* you would!'

Charlie wasn't a bit happy. He created a huge fuss, yowling and climbing up my legs.

'Ow!' I said. 'Shh! You'll wake the aunties!'

Eventually I shook him off, and he flounced into a corner in a sulk. I opened the window of my bedroom and climbed out into the night.

I made my way to St Munchin's through the deserted streets. It was deathly quiet. I wished I was tucked up in my own warm bed like everyone else instead of creeping through the night like a burglar. How did I get myself into these situations?

St Munchin's looked massive, black and scary

at night. The black iron gates were locked, so I squeezed through a gap in the fence into the playground. I knew that one of the windows of the corridor had a broken catch, so I crept along, testing each window.

Every time a branch creaked or a bird flapped, it felt like my heart leapt into my mouth. A nervous sweat broke out on my forehead and dribbled into my eyes. Finally I found the right window and climbed through it into the school.

The school corridor was even spookier than the playground. There were no lights on, but a full moon shone through the windows. The jagged shadows of the trees swayed black against the wall. They twisted as if dancing to wild music that no human could hear …

I crept to Mrs Winkle's room, held my breath and pushed open the door. My heart felt as if it was going to burst as I crept into her office and towards her desk.

There sat the silver box, glinting in a beautiful pool of magical moonlight.

I went to the top drawer in the desk. I opened it

– and there was the silver key! I hugged myself in excitement and picked it up. I tiptoed to the box and slotted the silver key inside the lock. The box sprang open at once.

The box was packed to the brim with magical objects, tricks and spells. Most of the stuff was out of my league – I wasn't even allowed to handle magic like this yet.

There was invisibility powder, giant finger bones for telling the future, magic dust, a mini-crystal ball, a dream kit, phials of dragon poison ...

I picked up an open jar full of green goo, sniffed it and recoiled. *Yuk!* It smelt like a cross between old fish guts and rancid camel's milk.

I looked at the label.

'"Sorcery Slime",' I read aloud. *Smelly* Slime more like! I put the jar on the desk and continued rummaging in the box.

I was so busy rifling about, I didn't see the extra shadow on the wall at first ...

But at the back of my neck the hairs stood on end. A dark shape appeared in the corner of my eye. I stopped, turned around slowly and squinted. It was a shadow – and it was definitely growing …

What *was* it – a tree branch, a cloud? The shadow grew bigger still. This was no tree. It had whiskers …

'Charlie? Is that you?' I whispered. I crossed my fingers. Maybe he'd ignored my instructions and followed me.

Suddenly the air was split by a piercing scream. My blood ran cold. I'd heard that sound before – and it wasn't Charlie!

Out of the gloom leapt the dark shape of Mrs Cuffy. She sprang onto the desk and fixed me with ratty little eyes full of hate. The next thing I knew, she had pushed me aside and jumped right into the magic box!

'Get out of there!' I shouted, trying to pull her out.

But Mrs Cuffy was surprisingly strong for a rat. She used one back leg to hold the box lid open and grabbed at the spells and potions with her two front paws. She picked up anything that came to hand – shrunken lizard heads, shark eyeballs, anything – and lobbed it at me.

There was nothing I could do except duck. I watched helplessly as magical objects whizzed out of the box, past my ears and all over the floor.

After about ten seconds, Mrs Cuffy's head popped above the side of the box. Her whiskers twitched as she held up something in her front paws. It was a test tube filled with pink powder. This time, she took careful aim before she threw it at me. I ducked out of the way of most of it, but a tiny bit scattered on my feet.

To my horror, my feet immediately went numb. I stared down at them. Inside my trainers, they grew smaller and smaller. As I lifted each one up to look, my socks and trainers fell off.

My mouth dropped open. On each foot my five toes had turned into two big toes and one small one! I rubbed my eyes hard.

I no longer had human feet – I had pig's trotters!

'Where are my feet?' I gasped. 'Mrs Cuffy! *What have you done to me?*'

I don't know if you've ever heard a rat

laughing but it is *not* a pretty sound. Mrs Cuffy clutched her sides as her furry, bony rat-shoulders shook with high-pitched giggles.

Furious, I grabbed the open jar of Sorcery Slime.

'Right, you horrible creature!' I shouted. 'Two can play at *that* game!'

I threw the green, smelly slime all over Mrs Cuffy.

For a moment, she froze like a statue, with her two front paws raised. Green gunk dripped off her fur. Then, right in front of my eyes, she changed – but not back into a human.

Instead, her snout grew longer and so did her yellow teeth.

Her tail shot out to twice its length and sprouted black bristles at the end.

Her body doubled to twice its normal size until she was the size of a dog. Her brown, greasy fur became shaggy and matted.

Within a few seconds, Mrs Cuffy had changed from an ordinary brown rat into a mutant monster – she was still a rat, but not like any rat I'd ever seen before. She was HUGE!

'Hell's teeth! What have I done now?' I whispered. I looked from Mrs Cuffy to my trotters and back again. 'I don't even think I can run away! I am *so* rat food!'

I backed into a corner as the monstrous Mrs Cuffy stalked towards me.

9

A LATE-NIGHT CONVERSATION

My heart beat louder and louder as Mrs Cuffy stalked closer and closer. Then her ears twitched once – and she stopped in her tracks. There was a noise outside the office.

It sounded like footsteps. I closed my eyes. Was it Mr Cuffy doing his rounds of the school? Or was it Mrs Winkle coming to collect her magic box? I didn't know which was worse – being caught burgling the head's office or becoming a late supper for a dog-sized rodent.

But Mrs Cuffy wasn't hanging around to see who was coming. She shot one last spite-filled look at me, and leapt towards the closed window. She crashed through it in a shower of splinters and was gone, leaving an enormous rat-shaped hole in the glass.

The footsteps in the hall paused for a second and then came straight towards the office. I was caught like a cockroach in a glue trap.

I snapped shut the lid of the magic box and threw the key in the drawer. I flung myself on the floor behind the desk and crouched down. The door creaked open.

But it wasn't Mr Cuffy or Mrs Winkle. Instead, peeping around the door, I saw the very *last* face I was expecting.

'*Mary*!' I said, standing up.

'Ha!' she said. 'Got you!'

'I can't believe it!' I said. 'What are *you* doing here?'

'I saw you climbing out your bedroom window and I followed you,' she said. 'Anyway, never mind about *me*! What are *you* up to? And why is there all this weird stuff on the floor?'

I didn't know where to start. I had never told Mary I was a witch in case she didn't want to be friends with me any more. But now, she'd caught me behaving very strangely indeed.

Maybe it was time I told the truth. I was so sick of lying. And, after all, Mary *was* my best friend.

But what if she didn't believe me? What if she thought I was mad or lying?

And what on earth was she going to say about my new feet? Who wanted to be best friends with a girl who had pig's trotters instead of toes?

'Mary,' I said. 'Sit down. I've got something to tell you.'

'You certainly have, madam!' she said, plonking herself in a chair and crossing her arms.

I took a deep breath and told Mary the whole story. Nearly.

She listened in silence as I told her how Aunty Grizz and Aunty Wormella had adopted me, and how we all found out I was a natural-born witch.

I told how about how I studied magic outside school hours. I told her all about shape-shifting and about what I'd done to Mrs Cuffy.

I told her about running into Mrs Cuffy this evening. Finally I showed her my hideous pig-feet.

On the whole, Mary took it pretty well. She went quiet for a second and stared at me. I held my breath. Would she gang up with other kids and tease me at school tomorrow?

'Wow, Anna!' she finally said as a smile crept across her face. 'That's *so* cool! I would never have guessed – you look so ordinary!'

She paused, looked at my trotters, and stifled a giggle.

'Well, *most* of you does, anyway!' she said.

'Thanks a lot!' I said.

'But where did all this stuff come from?' asked Mary, wrinkling her nose.

'They're potions of mine from home,' I lied. 'I store them in school sometimes.'

Although I could tell Mary everything about myself, I couldn't breathe a word about Mrs Winkle. That's a golden rule in witchcraft: one witch never tells on another.

'Can you walk, Anna?' asked Mary. 'We could stuff your socks into your trainers and jam your feet into them. They won't slip off and no one will notice!'

And that's when I knew it would be all right – that Mary was still on *my* side! My breath gushed out in a huge sigh of relief.

'Come on,' I said. 'Let's get going.'

All the way home we chatted about witchcraft. It felt great to share it all with someone. Back in the warm kitchen at number 13 Crag Road, we tried to decide what to do next.

'So the situation is,' said Mary, finishing her cocoa, 'that instead of having an ordinary rat to worry about, we've got a monster, mutant, killer, rodent on the loose.'

I hung my head. Charlie came and snuggled

between us and I tickled his ears.

'Not to mention,' she said, 'that you've got feet like a farm animal and you don't know how to get rid of them.'

'I keep trying to make things right,' I said. 'But instead I just make things worse!'

'Lucky for you that you've finally got some brains on board!' she said.

'I suppose that means you?' I said. 'Are you saying you'll help me?'

'Of course!' she said. 'We're friends, aren't we?'

I smiled for the first time in two days. Maybe things were looking up.

'Right,' I said. 'How are we going to find Mrs Cuffy again before she finds me?'

'Rats are creatures of habit,' said Mary. 'She'll probably keep hanging around the school, or somewhere else that's familiar.'

A lightbulb seemed to go on in my head.

'That's it!' I said. 'I bet she's near her old home! The Cuffys' house backs right onto the school. That's why she keeps popping up all over the place!'

'Yes, that makes sense,' said Mary. 'But what's she living on?'

'Didn't you tell me that rats scavenge food scraps?' I said. 'And the school kitchen dustbins are at the bottom of the Cuffys' garden! We'll start there!'

'Well done, genius,' yawned Mary. 'But what do we do with her when we find her? She's no longer your average rat, is she, not now that you've had another go at her.'

My shoulders slumped.

'I need to think about this,' I said. 'I need to get out my magic books and learn how to change that monster back into Mrs Cuffy. I admit I can shape-shift all right, but I'm not very good at changing things back.'

'So I see,' said Mary, yawning again. 'Can I go now? I *have* to get some sleep before school.'

'Lucky you,' I said, stretching my arms out. 'I've got too much to do to sleep. See you tomorrow?'

'Bye-bye, Porkers,' said Mary, grinning. I scowled.

Five minutes later, Charlie and I were on my bed in the attic surrounded by all my spell books. I was determined to stay awake all night and find a spell that would sort out Mrs Cuffy once and for all.

Two minutes after that, I was lying on top of the books, dribbling. I was fast asleep.

10

'AS YOU WERE'

Next morning, I got up early and crept around the house like a ghost. I could not let Aunty Grizz and Aunty Wormella see my horrible new feet, so I made my breakfast and got ready for school before they were up.

I jammed my feet into my wellies and wedged socks inside. Then I limped to school.

St Munchin's was in chaos. The new-style mutant rat was popping up all over the place and scaring everyone half to death. Mr Cuffy was stamping around in a fury, laying down poisoned traps and shouting at everyone.

'I'll kill that monster!' he roared. 'I'll get it, if it's the very last thing I do in this world!'

Owen Brady's gang had come to school armed with home-made catapults. Every time there

was a rustle behind a door or a table, they fired off soggy paper pellets.

They never hit Mrs Cuffy, of course – she was far too quick for them – but they hit each other and dozens of other kids. By lunchtime, the sick room was full to bursting with a steady stream of bruised, snivelling children.

Meanwhile, Mary and I flopped around like two wet rags. We were so tired that we couldn't take in anything. Luckily the school was in such an uproar that no one noticed. No one said anything about my wellies and we got away with doing nothing all day.

When the home-time bell rang, Mary lifted her head off her desk and woke up a bit.

'At last!' she said. 'So, are we going rat-hunting or what?'

'Sure you still want to come?' I said.

She shot me a withering look.

'Someone needs to keep an eye on you, don't they?' she said. 'Have you got your witchy kit with you? Let's have a look!'

I put my fingers to my lips. We waited until the last person had left class then I opened my bag.

'One black pointy hat,' I said. 'One genuine witch's wand, and one book of brilliant spells.'

But Mary was difficult to impress.

'That magic book looks a bit dog-eared,' she said, poking at it. 'Your hat's got a hole in it and your wand is bent!'

'It was all I could manage at short notice,' I said. 'Come on, let's go!'

We slipped out of class and followed the gravel path out of the school grounds to the bottom of the Cuffys' garden.

The big school bins were there all right. They

were overflowing with rubbish because the bin men hadn't been for a week – and, boy, did they *stink*!

'Here, ratty, ratty!' called Mary, holding her nose. 'Come on, there's a good girl!'

'She's not a *puppy*, Mary!' I said. 'And we've got to be quiet. She's *dangerous*, remember!' But Mary just giggled.

We searched around the bins. It was gross. The lids wouldn't close because there was a week's worth of rotting school dinners spilling out of the top of each bin. Flies and wasps buzzed around our heads as we poked around.

Suddenly Mary made a strangled sound, grabbed my arm and pointed upwards to the top of one of the bins.

Sure enough, there she was – Cuffy the monster rat!

Crouched on a pile of green, mouldy sausages, she looked even more enormous by daylight. She was gnawing hard at the rotting meat, and the black bristles on her greasy tail stood on end in pleasure.

I nudged Mary and put my finger to my lips. I opened my bag as quietly as I could, lifted out my witch hat and jammed it on my head. I whipped out the wand and spell book. I threw away the bag.

Mrs Cuffy's ears twitched but she continued chewing on the sausages. Keeping one eye on her, I picked up some twigs and made a magic star on the ground around me.

'Greedy pig,' whispered Mary, wrinkling her nose. 'No offence, Anna. I just mean she's so huge, she'll probably eat anything now.'

'She'll probably eat *us* if we stand still long enough!' I whispered. 'You'd better take cover.

This is the difficult bit.'

'Don't worry, I'm off!' said Mary. She shot behind the nearest bin and stayed there. Peeping out from the side, she gave me a thumbs-up.

I opened my spell book at a page near the back. The spell's title read: *As You Were*.

I raised my wand and drew a deep breath.

But before I had a chance to say anything, Mrs Cuffy's head shot up and her whiskers twitched. *Blast it*, I thought. *She's spotted me.*

But Mrs Cuffy wasn't looking at me. She was gazing straight past me over my shoulder. I heard a crunch on the gravel behind me. I spun around.

Mr Cuffy was standing on the path. He was holding a shotgun – and pointing it straight at Mrs Cuffy.

11

ANNA'S SPELL

'**O**ut of the way, missy, and you won't get hurt!' shouted Mr Cuffy.

I was so shocked at the sight of the school caretaker waving a gun about, that I dropped my spell book and my wand in a puddle. Mrs Cuffy's reaction was just as dramatic. When *she* saw Mr Cuffy, she stood up on her huge hind legs, held out her arms and whimpered.

Mr Cuffy raised his gun and my heart nearly stopped.

'NO, Mr Cuffy!' I shouted. 'You can't! You can't *kill* her!'

'That's what you think!' he shouted. 'I'll not let it escape a second time! Move yourself, girly! NOW!'

'But you don't understand!' I pleaded. 'That

rat – she's your *wife*!'

Mr Cuffy's eyes swivelled towards me. His red face went dark purple and the veins in his forehead stood out so much they looked as though they would pop.

'I *beg* your pardon!' he shouted. 'How *dare* you!'

For a moment I thought he was going to shoot *me* instead of Mrs Cuffy! I covered my face with my hands. Mr Cuffy struggled to control his temper.

'No one gets the better of Joe Cuffy,' he hissed, stamping down the path towards the bins. 'Animal, human – or child!'

By now, Mrs Cuffy was leaping up and down on the rubbish, wagging her finger at Mr Cuffy and squealing at the top of her thin, ratty voice. Mr Cuffy looked confused for a moment. It was as if the rat reminded him of someone …

Then he shook his head, raised the shotgun to his shoulder again and placed his finger on the trigger.

'Say your prayers, rodent!' he said. Slowly his

finger started to squeeze the trigger.

Mrs Cuffy stopped jumping and froze on the spot. Her beady black eyes swivelled from her husband to me and back again. Was it my imagination, or was she asking for help ...?

I had to act, and act fast. I scrambled to my feet and jumped back inside my magic star. I couldn't read my book of spells because it was soaked and filthy. So I pointed one index finger Mrs Cuffy and one at Mr Cuffy and made up a rhyme on the spot:

'Mr Cuffy, spare her life,
Don't pull the trigger on your wife!
Mrs C, though you've been bad,
Resume the human form you had –
BUT one thing more before you start:
You'll both FORGET about my part!'

The seconds ticked by. I held my breath. Everyone seemed frozen in time.

Then Mrs Cuffy unfroze herself, spat a bit of mouldy sausage at me and began to climb down

the side of the bin. She was still a rat!

Meanwhile Mr Cuffy unfroze *him*self, shot me a dirty look and raised his gun again.

'Don't give up, Anna!' shouted Mary. Her face, peering around the bin, was hopeful and both her thumbs were raised in a sign of good luck. 'One more time!' she shouted.

I did the rhyme again – but this time, at the top of my voice.

At last, I felt the magic power surging through my legs, into my arms, and flowing out through my fingers towards Mr and Mrs Cuffy. There was a flash of blue flame and a deafening bang.

When the smoke cleared, a grimy, greasy HUMAN Mrs Cuffy was clinging to the side of the rubbish bin! Mr Cuffy's mouth was open and his gun was on the ground. He goggled at his wife.

'What the …' he whispered. 'Edel?'

'Joey!' shouted Mrs Cuffy, reaching out both arms to her husband and crashing to the ground. Mr Cuffy raced forward to his wife and dragged her to her feet.

'Edel? Is that

really you?' he said. 'Look at the state of you! Where on earth have you *been*?'

'I don't know, Joey!' whimpered Mrs Cuffy.

'What do you mean, *you don't know*!' shouted Mr Cuffy. He looked around him. 'And where's that blasted rat?'

'What rat, Joey?' said Mrs Cuffy. She looked down at herself. 'Why do I look like this? *What's been happening*?'

Mary and I exchanged glances. I edged over to her hiding place.

'Time for us to push off, I think,' I said.

Mary nodded and broke into a huge dimpled smile. We slunk into the bushes and headed for home.

12

'FIRM, BUT FAIR'

The next morning the whole school echoed to the sounds of Mr Cuffy complaining that Mrs Winkle had taken his gun away. He was also very suspicious of Mrs Cuffy, who couldn't remember a thing about where she'd been for three days. As for the huge rat, he simply couldn't understand what had happened to it.

Meanwhile, Mrs Cuffy was taken down to the police station and told off for disappearing and wasting police time.

By now I felt pretty sorry for them both. Soon I felt so guilty that I found myself outside Mrs Winkle's office ready to confess everything – and ask for help with my own little problem.

'Come in, Anna Kelly!' shouted Mrs Winkle

before I'd even knocked. I took a deep breath and entered.

'Well, well, well,' said Mrs Winkle. 'If it isn't our very own trainee witch – and part-time burglar!'

She peered over her glasses, and her piercing blue gaze skewered me to the floor. Everything in the office was neat and tidy as usual and the broken window had already been replaced. There was no sign of the magic box.

'I – I've come to apologise, Mrs Winkle,' I said. 'You were right all along. It *was* me who turned Mrs Cuffy into a rat in the first place – right here in school!'

'I knew it!' said Mrs Winkle, rapping the desk with her knuckles. 'And yet you looked me straight in the eye and lied about it!'

'I know,' I mumbled, very ashamed. 'I was trying to wriggle out of trouble.'

'And how did you get into my magic box?' said Mrs Winkle.

'I stole the key,' I said. 'Then I had a fight with Mrs Cuffy, which got a bit messy. It was me who wasted all the Sorcery Slime.'

'Do you know how difficult it is to make that stuff?' said Mrs Winkle. 'You have to milk beetles – it takes *weeks*!'

I looked up.

'And there's one other thing,' I said. 'I've told Mary Maxwell that I'm a witch!'

'*You did what*?' said Mrs Winkle, rising from behind her desk and pacing the floor. 'This is getting worse and worse.'

'I'm sorry,' I said.

'You'll have to be punished, you know,' said Mrs Winkle.

'Yes, I know,' I said, sighing. 'But I think it's

already started.'

I kicked off my wellies and peeled off my socks. My piggy-feet looked hideous.

Mrs Winkle put her fingers over her lips as if to stifle a laugh.

'Yes, I see what you mean,' she said. 'That'll be the Pinky Porker Powder that was scattered all over the carpet, right?'

'Yes, Miss,' I said.

'Anna, that's a taste of your own medicine. I want you to remember how it feels!' said Mrs Winkle. 'In future, you *never* use magic to settle scores with people you don't like!'

'Yes, Miss,' I said.

'*Or* lie to your superiors!' she said.

'Yes, Miss,' I said.

'*Or* broadcast your powers to the world!' she said.

'It will never happen again, Miss.'

Mrs Winkle sat down.

'Now. Your punishments,' she said. 'Firstly, I will speak to your aunts and make sure you are grounded for the rest of term!'

I sighed. I was expecting that one.

'Secondly,' she said. 'You will spend every evening for the next two weeks making more Sorcery Slime to replace what you wasted.'

Two weeks up to my eyes in beetles. Great.

'Yes, Miss,' I said, trying to sound chirpy about it.

'Thirdly, you will put a strong Forgetting Spell on Mary Maxwell,' said Mrs Winkle. 'She must remember nothing about your little adventure. Is that clear?'

I felt tears pricking my eyes. I hadn't realised how lonely it was keeping my secret all to myself until I had told Mary. I clasped my hands together and gazed up at Mrs Winkle.

'Please, Miss,' I said. 'I trust Mary! She's my best friend – she would *never* do anything to harm me! I'll do anything else you want – but please, *please* can't she know who and what I am!'

Mrs Winkle gazed at me steadily for a moment and drummed on the desk with her long fingers.

'Will you take another punishment instead?'

she said. '*Any* other punishment?'

This was risky. Who knew what Mrs Winkle was going to come out with! I dried my eyes and took a deep breath.

'Yes, Miss,' I said in a small, wobbly voice.

Mrs Winkle leapt out of her seat and pointed at me. I gasped. The wand in her hand had appeared out of nowhere.

'How about if I turned the rest of you into a pig – let's say for a *month*!' she boomed. 'And see how *you* like it!'

I blinked and swallowed hard. Life as a pig! Was I really ready to pay such a high price for my friendship with Mary?

'OK, Miss,' I whispered. 'Whatever you say!'

Mrs Winkle raised her arms high. We stood looking at each other without blinking for a long moment, but the spell that trembled on her lips never came. Her blue eyes softened, she lowered her arms and sat down.

'I'm not made of stone, Anna,' she said. 'I know being a witch can be a lonely business sometimes. I'll allow Mary Maxwell to keep your secret. But in return you will do something else. You will help Mrs Cuffy in the science lab every morning before school for the rest of term – and learn to get along with her!'

I heaved a deep sigh and nodded. Firm, but fair – that's what they called Mrs Winkle. And I had to admit it was true. I wasn't looking forward to the next few weeks – but I had certainly learned my lesson about using my powers in the right way.

'Do you agree with this plan, Anna?' said Mrs Winkle.

'Yes, Miss,' I said.

'Right, sign here, please,' she said, whipping out a sheet of paper from her desk.

I read through the paper. It was a contract stating all the things I had promised to do. Mrs Winkle certainly wasn't taking any chances. I signed my name at the bottom.

'Finished?' said Mrs Winkle. She smiled and clicked her fingers. 'You can put your shoes and socks on now.'

I bent down to grab my shoes and socks and

gasped. Instead of the pig's trotters, I was looking at my own two familiar feet! I was no longer
part-pig – I was human again!

'See how good it feels to be a human?' said Mrs
Winkle. 'Remember that, Anna Kelly!'

I felt a massive weight lift off my shoulders.

'Yes, Miss! I shouted. 'Thanks, Miss!'

I was free! I turned and raced out of the office. Outside in the sunny playground, Mary and the other kids were playing football.

HAVE YOU READ ANNA'S OTHER ADVENTURES?

TURN THE PAGE TO READ MORE!

LEAVING SUNNY HILLS

I couldn't believe my eyes when I first saw number 13 Crag Road. No wonder everyone at the Sunny Hills Children's Home had sniggered when I'd said it was going to be my new home.

Everything about number 13 was crooked. Its walls were crooked, its chimneys were crooked. Even its doors and windows were crooked.

It looked like it was going to fall over any second.

But crooked or not, number 13 was my new home. You see, the two ladies who owned the place, Grizz and Wormella Mint, had adopted me.

My name's Anna Kelly. I don't have any parents, and I have never had a proper home. I've been at Sunny Hills Children's Home since I was a tiny baby. By the time I was nine, so many people had decided NOT to adopt me that I had grown used to the idea of spending the rest of my life at Sunny Hills.

But I wasn't happy about it, not one bit. So when Grizz and Wormella turned up, promising me a pink-and-white bedroom with its own private bathroom, a posh new school, new clothes, weekly pocket money and my own TV, I felt like I'd won the Lotto!

They had been *so* sweet in Mrs Pegg's office. *So* sweet and *so* keen to have me. Very, very keen.

'Anna, darling,' the skinny one had cooed. 'You'll have the run of the house! You'll be able to do exactly as you like!'

'Thanks, Miss!' I said.

'Call me "aunty", dear,' she crooned.

The run of the house! Able to do what I wanted! That suited me just fine. I was used to a lot of rules and regulations at Sunny Hills. It was porridge at 7.00am, lights out at 9.00pm, that kind of thing.

But *now*! Now life was looking up! The two old dears' only wish was to pamper me. I'd get new clothes, new toys …

It took exactly a minute after arriving at number 13 Crag Road for me to realise I'd made a mistake. A big, BIG mistake.

The Witch Apprentice by Marian Broderick, ISBN 978-1-84717-129-0

MRS WINKLE GETS CROSS

You're going to a witches' workshop this Saturday,' said Mrs Winkle.

'*This* Saturday?' I said. 'But I can't *this* Saturday, Miss!'

'What do you mean, you can't?' said Mrs Winkle, frowning. 'It's all arranged.'

'I'm really sorry, Miss,' I said. 'But Mary and I are having a sleepover at my house. We've been planning it for ages ...'

'A *sleepover*?' said Mrs Winkle. 'Sitting around watching rubbish on TV and eating junk food? Do you really think *that's* more important than working on your magic?'

That was exactly what I thought – but I didn't dare say so. So I just stared at the floor and moved from one foot to the other.

'Stubborn child!' she said. 'You must at least promise you'll practise at home this weekend,' she said. 'A *lot*. Sleepover or not!'

'Yes, Miss,' I said. 'I promise.'

In the playground, Mary was leaning against the old hazel tree.

'What was all *that* about?' she said.

'Nothing,' I said. 'Homework lecture, that's all.'

'Come on,' said Mary. 'Let's go home by Coldwell Wood, it'll be quicker!'

A shiver ran down my spine.

'Do we have to?' I said. 'It's safer by the main road.'

'Don't be such a baby!' said Mary. 'Last one to Crag Road is a turnip!' She shot off into the trees.

I hesitated. I always avoid dark, creepy places. You never knew who – or what – you might meet. But I could see Mary's blue school jumper disappearing into the gloom. So I hoicked my bag over my shoulder, and jogged into the wood after her.

'Let's at least stick to the path, OK?' I panted, as I fell into step beside her.

'Yes, Grandma,' said Mary. 'Keep your freckles on.'

We strolled along in silence. The dry leaves crackled beneath our feet and somewhere a bird squawked.

'Listen to that!' I said. 'It sounds like a cat being turned inside out!'

'Sounds more like you in choir today!' said Mary.

'Hey!' I laughed and slapped her arm.

Mary danced out of reach, giggling.

'Come on then!' she sang. 'Come and get me!'

She ran between two huge oak trees and into the dark wood.

I groaned.

'Mary!' I said. 'Stop it! You'll get us in trouble!'

I stopped walking. There was dead silence.

'Mary!' I shouted. I could hear my own voice quavering. 'Mary?'

Keep walking, I told myself. *Mary's all right, she's just messing about.*

But I couldn't walk. All I could do was stare into the trees, where Mary had disappeared.

Between the two oaks, I could see a glimmering green light – and it was growing brighter and brighter.

The Witch in the Woods by Marian Broderick, ISBN 978-1-84717-108-5